MONKEY

A TRICKSTER TALE FROM INDIA

Gerald McDermott

Houghton Mifflin Harcourt

Boston New York

All rights reserved. Originally published in hardcover in the
United States by Harcourt Children's Books, an imprint of
Houghton Mifflin Harcourt Publishing Company, 2011.

For information about permission to reproduce selections from this book, write to
trade.permissions@hmhco.com or to Permissions, Houghton Mifflin Harcourt
Publishing Company, 3 Park Avenue, 19th Floor, New York, New York 10016.

The illustrations in this book were created with textured papers
hand-colored by the artist with fabric paint and ink,
then mounted on heavy watercolor paper.

The text type was set in Goudy Sans Bold.
The display lettering was created by Gerald McDermott.
Designed by Gerald McDermott and Judyth Sieck.

Library of Congress Cataloging-in-Publication Data
McDermott, Gerald.
Monkey: a trickster tale from India/by Gerald McDermott
p. cm.
Summary: Crocodile wants to feast on Monkey's heart and
Monkey must outsmart him if he is to enjoy eating mangoes all day.
[1. Folklore—India.] I. Title.
PZ8.1.M159Mon 2010
398.2—dc22
[E]
2009007977

www.hmhco.com

ISBN: 978-0-15-216596-3 hardcover
ISBN: 978-0-544-33918-7 paperback

Manufactured in China
SCP 10 9 8
4500750863

The tale of clever Monkey and dull-witted Crocodile is from the Buddhist tradition. The story is part of an ancient collection of folklore, fables, and legends called the Jataka tales, which originated in India in the third and fourth centuries B.C. and circulated throughout Southeast Asia for thousands of years. Translated from the original Sanskrit into English in the nineteenth century, most notably by W. H. D. Rouse in his 1895 work for the University of Cambridge Press, the 547 stories have since been published in countless editions in many languages.

For this final volume in my series of six trickster tales, I was inspired to tell this popular story—known as the Sumsumara-Jataka—because of its wonderful mixture of morality and irony. It is Monkey who has the "heart" that Crocodile lacks, and brute force cannot prevail. The playfulness of the story lent itself to a bold collage of cut and torn papers, some from India and Southeast Asia. The floral design on the cover, commonly referred to in the West as paisley, is known throughout India as the "raw mango" motif and is the basis for a key element in my telling.

I'm grateful to Sujata Shahane for her valuable suggestions and to her remarkable daughters, Rhea and Tanvi, for their enthusiastic support. My gratitude, as well, goes to book artist Tania Baban-Natal for sharing the technique of teasing apart moistened handmade paper to create a furry edge. Finally, deep thanks to my editor, Jeannette Larson, paragon of perceptiveness and patience.

—G.M.

For Mallory, Hannah, and Tanner

Monkey!

Chattering Monkey.
He lived high in a tree on the banks
of the wide, flowing river.

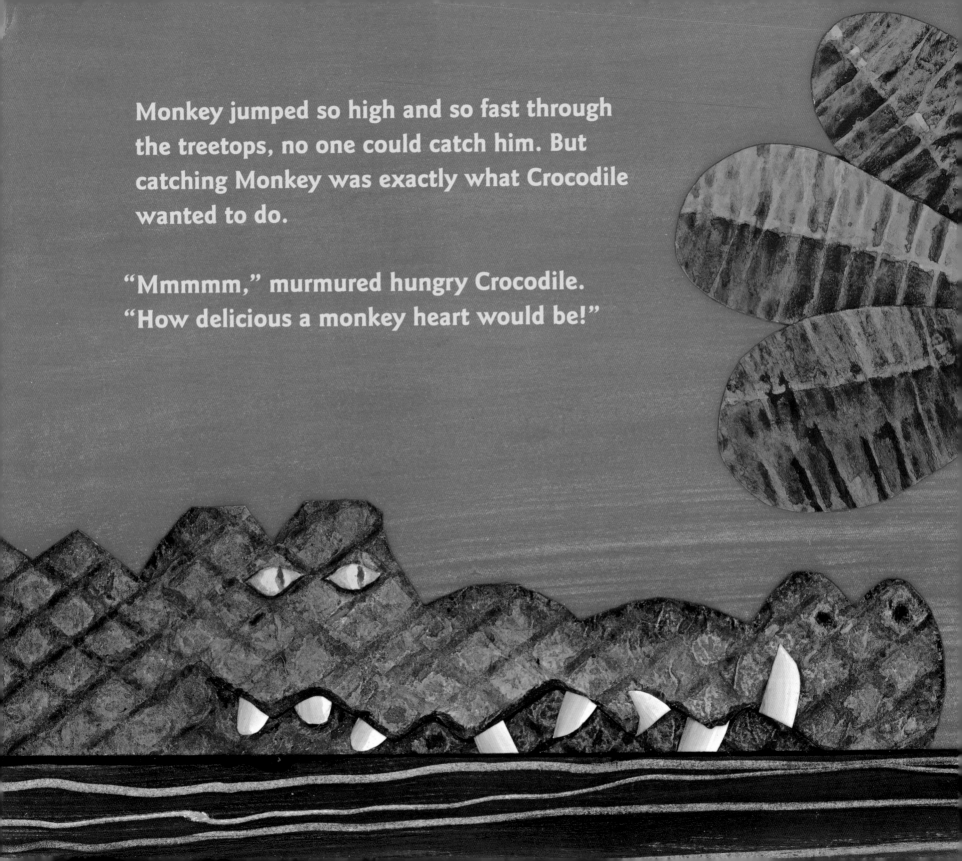

Monkey jumped so high and so fast through the treetops, no one could catch him. But catching Monkey was exactly what Crocodile wanted to do.

"Mmmmm," murmured hungry Crocodile. "How delicious a monkey heart would be!"

Crocodile slithered into the water.
"Good morning, Monkey!" he called out.

"Good morning, Crocodile!" answered Monkey.
"Where are you going?"

"To the island in the middle of the river,"
answered Crocodile.

"Yum," said Monkey. "Delicious mangoes grow there, but that's too far for me to swing."

"Climb on my back, my friend," called Crocodile. "I'll take you to the island."

Monkey swung down from the tree
and hopped onto Crocodile's scaly back.

As Crocodile glided through the deep,
dark water, he sank lower and lower.

Monkey began to get wet.

"Oh, my goodness—I cannot swim!" shouted Monkey.

"How well I know," said Crocodile. "Now I'm going to eat your heart!"

"Eat my heart?" said Monkey. "What a pity. I left it up in the tree!"

"You left your heart in the tree?" Crocodile grumbled. "What a nuisance."

Crocodile returned with Monkey
to the muddy brown riverbank.
As soon as they reached the
shore, Monkey leaped off
Crocodile's back and scampered
up a tall tree, laughing
and chattering.

'Look, my heart is here!"
called Monkey from the treetop.
'Just climb up and get it!"

Crocodile grunted and thrashed
and swam away.

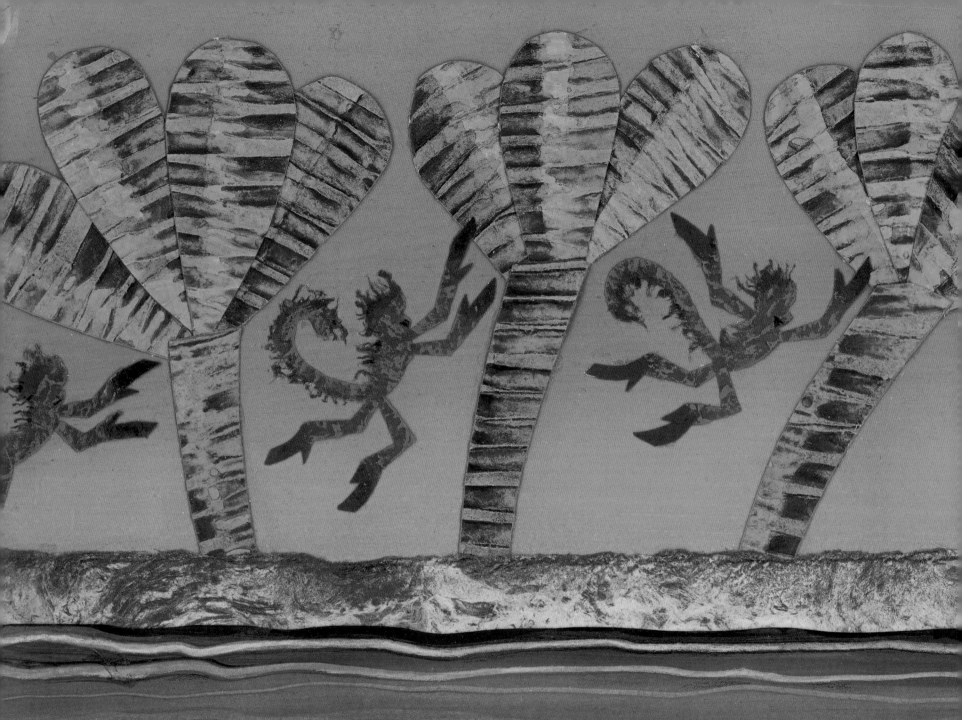

Now Monkey wanted the delicious mangoes more than ever. He leaped from treetop to treetop until he discovered some large rocks far downriver.

He saw that if he skipped across the rocks to the island, he could feast on mangoes every day.

The next morning, Crocodile came swimming
down the river, looking for Monkey.

He heard Monkey chattering. He saw
Monkey jump from tree to rock to island.

"I shall pretend I'm a rock," said Crocodile.
"When Monkey jumps on me, I will snap him up,
heart and all!"

Crocodile lay low in the water all day long.

When Monkey had eaten his fill, he headed for home with all the mangoes he could carry. He jumped off the island onto a rock in the river. He was about to jump onto another rock, but something was wrong.

Monkey looked closer, then called out in a cheery voice, "Hello, Rock!"

Crocodile was silent. He lay low in the water.

Monkey called out again. "I say, good evening, Rock!"

Crocodile said nothing.

"Rock, will you not greet me this evening?" asked Monkey.

Crocodile thought the rock must usually answer. He said, "Good evening."

"Ha! You're not Rock!" said Monkey. "You're Crocodile!"

"I'm as good as a rock," said Crocodile. "You can jump on me to get to the other side."

"Oh, what a splendid idea!" said Monkey. "Here I come!"

Monkey got ready to leap. Crocodile closed his eyes and opened his jaws.

But instead of leaping, Monkey popped
a mango right into Crocodile's mouth.

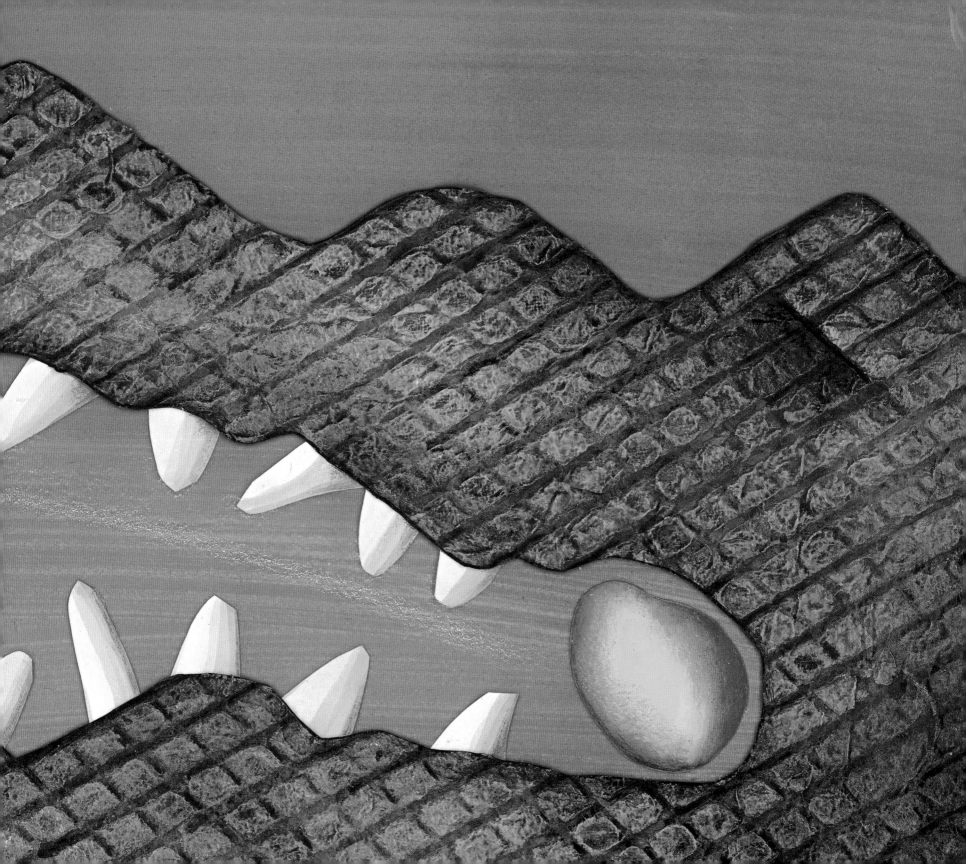

Bang! Crocodile snapped his jaws shut.

Quickly, Monkey jumped on Crocodile's nose,
then onto the muddy brown riverbank.

Laughing and chattering, Monkey scampered
up a tree and swung from branch to branch.

"Your teeth may be sharp,"
Monkey shouted to Crocodile.
"But your mind is dull!"

Now Monkey feasts on
delicious mangoes every day.

Crocodile lies low in the
water, keeping an eye on him.

And when Monkey crosses
the river to go home,
he is always careful
to jump on a rock,
not on a crocodile.